THE
UNOFFICIAL
JOKE BOOK
FOR FANS OF
HARRY POTTER

THE UNOFFICIAL JOKE BOOK FOR FANS OF HARRY POTTER

VOL. 1

BRIAN BOONE

ILLUSTRATIONS BY

AMANDA BRACK

Sky Pony Press
New York

Sky Pony Press books may be purchased in bulk at special discounts for sales promotion, corporate gifts, fund-raising, or educational purposes. Special editions can also be created to specifications. For details, contact the Special Sales Department, Sky Pony Press, 307 West 36th Street, 11th Floor, New York, NY 10018 or info@skyhorsepublishing.com.

Sky Pony® is a registered trademark of Skyhorse Publishing, Inc.®, a Delaware corporation.

Visit our website at www.skyponypress.com.

10 9 8 7 6 5

Library of Congress Cataloging-in-Publication Data is available on file.

Cover artwork: iStockphoto/Shutterstock

Box Set ISBN: 978-1-5107-4816-3
Ebook ISBN: 978-1-5107-4817-0

Printed in China

CONTENTS

Introduction

Like millions of other lucky readers, you've likely been completely enchanted by the wizarding world developed by J.K. Rowling over the course of seven classic *Harry Potter* novels. And who can blame you? It's a marvelous place full of action, adventure, spells, potions, hexes, amazing creatures, and magical places—like Hogwarts School of Witchcraft and Wizardry—where absolutely anything is possible.

You've probably got your own magic wand; you know which Hogwarts house you've been sorted into, and you may even have your *patronus* figured out. In short, you're a hardcore Potterhead. And now it's time to laugh it up with *The Unofficial Harry Potter Joke Book*. While Rowling's books—and the great movies made from them—are completely engrossing, the one thing they're not is laugh-out-loud funny. Here's where *we* bring the magic. *The Unofficial Harry Potter Joke Book* is fuller than Dumbledore's Pensieve, loaded with hundreds of jokes that poke a little fun at wizards, witches, Hogwarts, Voldemort, Ron, Hermione, Snape, Hagrid, and, of course, the Boy Who Lived himself. Quidditch quips? Score! Slytherin sillies and Ravenclaw ha-ha's? Huzzah! Cracks at the expense of He Who Must Not Be Named? *Always.*

One thing is for sure: with *The Unofficial Harry Potter Joke Book,* you can *expecto laughs.*

CHAPTER 1

HARRY, HERMIONE, RON, AND OTHER STUDENTS OF MAGIC

Q. What did Harry and Ron have in common when they met?

A. One had a scar, and the other had Scabbers.

•

Q. Where do Hermione's parents live?

A. Back home on the Grange!

Q. Do you know what Hermione's patronus is?
A. Well, you otter.

Q. Do you know what Ron's patronus is then?
A. It would be terrier if you didn't!

●

Q. Why did Harry move?
A. He didn't like the cabinets.

Q. What do wizards and fish have in common?
A. They hang out in schools.

●

Q. Why did Draco avoid Hermione the first time they met?
A. His parents told him to never talk to Grangers.

●

Q. What do you get when you cross a Ravenclaw with the infirmary?
A. Ill-literacy

●

Q. What's a Slytherin's favorite subject?
A. Hisssssstory.

●

Q. Why are Slytherin's house colors green and black?
A. Because red and gold were already taken!

●

Q. Why are Gryffindor's house colors red and gold?
A. Because red and pink don't look very good together.

Q. Did you hear about Percy Weasley?

A. His mother said he was the perfect prefect!

•

Q. Why was Hermione such a good student?

A. Where there's a quill, there's a way!

•

Q. Why did Ron have such a hard time studying?

A. He lacked hocus focus.

•

Q. Did you hear about the first-year who returned his house tie?

A. He said it was too tight.

•

Q. Where does Harry Potter buy furniture?

A. At the Harry Pottery Barn.

•

Q. What do Marauders do at night when everybody's tired?

A. They take a Map!

4

Q. Where do Hogwarts students leave their complaints?
A. In the Goblet of Ire.

•

Q. What's the one class Hogwarts somehow doesn't have?
A. Spelling.

•

Q. How are new students like birds?
A. They have to learn Flying.

•

Q. How does Harry's best friend get his exercise?
A. He Rons.

•

Q. Why didn't Harry like the Triwizard Tournament?
A. It was dragon on and on.

•

Q. What do you call a star pupil in Professor Sprout's class?
A. "Herb."

Q. What do a potions pot and Harry's best friend have in common?

A. They're both cauldron.

●

Q. Once again, Draco's plan to get Potter was ruined.

A. He was Malfoyled!

●

Q. How do the Malfoys enter a building?

A. They Slytherin.

●

Q. Why did the wizard drop out of Hogwarts to travel the world?

A. She had wand-erlust.

●

Q. Did you hear about the Hogwarts student from outer space?

A. He was a flying sorcerer.

Q. What do you call a Hufflepuff who works in a casino?
A. A Shufflepuff.

•

Q. What do you call a Hufflepuff who makes fancy chocolate?
A. A Trufflepuff.

•

Q. What do you call a Hufflepuff who makes dresses?
A. A Rufflepuff.

•

Q. What do you call a Hufflepuff who works in a mechanic's shop?
A. A Mufflerpuff.

•

Q. What do you call a Hufflepuff who gets into fights?
A. A Scufflepuff.

Q. What do you call a Hufflepuff who always has a big bag of stuff with them?

A. Dufflepuff.

Q. What's one thing Hogwarts students have to look out for?

A. Desk Eaters.

•

Q. Why did Crabbe and Goyle cross the road?

A. Because Draco told them to.

Q. Why do Slytherins cross the road twice?

A. Because they are double-crossers.

•

Q. Why was Luna such a good friend?

A. Because Luna Lovegood.

•

Q. Why did Neville never have a problem finding a place to sit?

A. Because of his Longbottom.

•

Q. What is Ron at Christmas?

A. A sweater-getter.

Q. When is Ron not called Ron?
A. When he's Cauldron Cakes.

●

Q. What's Bill Weasley's favorite flower?
A. Fleur!

●

Q. At least at first, did Cedric like being in the Triwizard Tournament?
A. Yeah, he could really Diggory it!

●

Q. What does a Hufflepuff do after a wand duel?
A. He huffs and puffs!

●

Q. Into what house do grumpy wizards get sorted?
A. Grumblepuff.

●

Q. Who's the most popular rapper in the wizarding world?
A. Man-Drake.

Q. What do wizards put on their ice cream?
A. Magic Shell.

•

Q. What did Snape say when Harry fell into a prickly blackberry bush?
A. "Points, Gryffindor!"

•

Q. Why did Malfoy get mad in Potions?
A. He reached his boiling point.

•

Q. Which house throws the best parties?
A. Ravin' Claw.

•

Q. Why did Crabbe want to go to the Yule Ball?
A. He knew a Goyle that was going.

•

Q. Why were they called Dumbledore's Army?
A. Because they didn't have the boats to be Dumbledore's Navy.

11

Q. What would a book about Harry's best friend be called?

A. A Ronicle.

•

Q. Why did the Slytherin get a job at the post office?

A. They liked that he could speak parseltongue.

•

Q. Where does Hermione learn everything she knows?

A. Witchipedia.

•

Q. Why didn't the professors like having twins Padma and Parvati Patil at Hogwarts?

A. They never knew which witch was which.

•

Q. Why was Draco's shirt so dirty?

A. He spent the day in Slytherin in the mud.

Q. What do Harry Potter and Charlie Brown have in common?

A. They're both in love with the little girl with red hair.

●

"Any fools in the room, please stand up," Professor Snape said sarcastically. After some silence, a first year stood up.

"So, then you consider yourself a fool, do you?" asked Professor Snape.

"Not really," said the student, "but I didn't want to see you standing up there all by yourself."

●

Q. What's the one book Hermione never needed to read?

A. The dictionary—she's an excellent speller!

●

Q. Why did Draco's best friend yell at him?

A. He was feeling Crabbey.

Q. Why didn't the student from Durmstrang want to compete in the Triwizard Tournament?

A. He was feeling Krummy.

•

Q. Where can you find Dumbledore's Army?

A. In Dumbledore's sleevy!

•

Q. Why couldn't the Slytherin talk to snakes yet?

A. He was still waiting for the arrival of his parcel-tongue!

•

Q. What's the worst day to go into the girl's bathroom at Hogwarts?

A. On Moan-day.

•

Q. What did Viktor say to Hermione when he took her to the Yule Ball?

A. "You look bewitching!"

Q. Did you hear that Hermione used a Time-Turner to go back in time and give socks to almost 10 house elves?

A. It's true—a witch in time saved nine!

•

Q. What do you call the standard Hogwarts uniform pants?

A. Witches' britches.

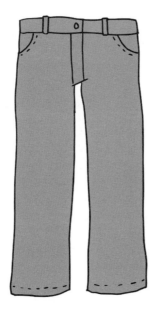

Q. Who was on the Hogwarts Inquisitorial Squad?
A. Why do you need to know that, hmm?

•

Q. What's the difference between Dumbledore's phoenix and Seamus Finnigan's patronus?
A. One is Fawkes, and the other is a fox.

•

Q. Did you hear about the powerful wizards that had to duel?
A. It was a case of wand-to-wand combat!

•

Q. What kind of glasses does Moaning Myrtle wear?
A. Spooktacles.

•

Q. Why doesn't Hogwarts have a basketball team?
A. They did once, but the team could only score 9 in 3 quarters.

Q. What did Draco tell his father?

A. Everything!

•

Q. What was Hermione when she married Ron?

A. A hitched witch!

Chapter 2

PROFESSORS AND OTHER MAGICAL AUTHORITIES

Q. What's the difference between Dumbledore and a Hogwarts ghost?

A. One is the headmaster, and the other is headless.

•

Q. Why did everybody want to take Professor Flitwick's class?

A. Because he was so "charming."

•

Q. Why was Mad-Eye Moody such a bad teacher?

A. Because he can't control his pupils.

•

Q. What kind of fish is on the Divination teacher's face?

A. A Seer chin.

Q. What's the most charming thing not found in charms class?

A. Gilderoy Lockhart

•

Q. Did you hear about yet another magical creature on the grounds at Hogwarts?

A. It's positively Hagridiculous!

•

Q. Which Hogwarts professor gets blamed for everything?

A. Professor Snape Goat.

Q. What do you call a Headmaster of Hogwarts who doesn't speak clearly?

A. Mumbledore.

●

Q. What do you call a Headmaster of Hogwarts who keeps tripping on his cloak?

A. Stumbledore.

●

Q. Ron's grades were so bad that at least Snape didn't think he was doing what?

A. Cheating!

●

Q. What does the Potions teacher drink?

A. Snapele.

●

Q. What do you call a Hogwarts teacher with a bad attitude?

A. Moody!

Q. What does Professor Moody eat on a hot day?
A. Eye scream.

●

Q. What's Professor Lupin's favorite day of the week?
A. Moonday.

●

Q. Where does Professor Lupin live?
A. In a were-house.

●

Q. Why did Professor Quirrell have a hard time making friends?
A. He was all wrapped up with Voldemort.

●

Q. Why didn't Harry argue with the Defense Against the Dark Arts teacher?
A. He didn't want to Quirrell.

Q. Did you hear that the Hogwarts flying instructor kept dogs?

A. They were Hooch's pooches.

•

Q. How does Snape make raisins?

A. With Snape's grapes.

•

Q. What's a Potions teacher's favorite social media program?

A. Snapechat.

22

Professors and Other Magical Authorities

Q. Where does Professor Quirrell shop?

A. Turban Outfitters.

●

Professor Quirrell walks into the Hog's Head Inn, unwraps
  his turban, and presents the Dark Lord's face to the
  barman. The Dark Lord orders a Pumpkin Juice.
"Sorry, can't serve you," the barman says.
"What are you, out of your head?"

●

Q. Why couldn't Harry trust Professor Quirrell?

A. Because he was two-faced.

●

**Q. Did Nearly Headless Nick do well when he was a
  student at Hogwarts?**

A. Yes—he was nearly Head Boy!

●

Q. Where does Barty Crouch sleep?

A. On a Barty Couch.

Q. How does Barty hide?

A. He Crouches.

•

Q. Why couldn't Hogwarts students wear black-soled shoes?

A. Because Filch got mad about all the dark marks.

•

Q. What was the textbook in xylomancy?

A. Wooden you like to know.

•

Q. Did you hear about Professor Babbling's class?

A. It was runed.

•

Q. Did you hear about Professor Trelawney's class?

A. It was divine.

•

Q. Why does Moaning Myrtle sob?

A. You'd cry too if you had to spend eternity in a school bathroom.

Q. Did you hear about the horse who got expelled from Hogwarts?

A. He was a one-trick pony.

•

Q. Did you hear Hagrid's half-brother got lost in the forest for a while?

A. He lost his Grawp!

25

Q. Did you hear that Professor McGonagall stood up to Dolores Umbridge?

A. Yep, she had a lot of Minerva!

●

Q. What's a class with Professor Lockhart like?

A. You get class credit from the guy who classlessly stole credit!

●

Q. What's the difference between Gilderoy Lockhart and Ron's dad?

A. One is an author and the other is an Arthur.

●

Q. Why did Gilderoy Lockhart team up with Nearly Headless Nick?

A. He needed a ghost-writer.

●

Q. What professor can't remember the questions she wants to ask?

A. Professor Ummmmmmmbridge.

Q. Did you hear the Hogwarts headmaster is a talented percussionist?

A. They used to call him Drumbledore!

•

Q. Why didn't Dumbledore take the train?

A. He preferred the Albus.

•

Q. Did you hear that a Hogwarts professor had to go to St. Mungo's?

A. He had a staff infection.

•

Q. Why did Professor Trelawney only predict sad events?

A. She was using a crystal bawl.

•

Q. Why did Professor Sprout take the Herbology job?

A. She wanted to get back to her roots.

•

Q. Did you hear Professor Sprout had a class at another wizarding school?

A. It was a branch office.

Q. What's Professor Sprout's favorite magazine?

A. *Weeder's Digest.*

Q. What are Snape's favorite flowers?

A. Lilies.

•

Q. Did you hear that Professor McGonagall's animagi and Crookshanks get together and gossip about students?

A. They're very catty.

Q. How many Snapes is more than a few?

A. Severus.

•

Q. Did you hear about the rumor that Snape is an evil wizard?

A. Yeah, they're pretty Severus.

•

Q. Why did Snape stand in the middle of the road?

A. So no one could tell what side he's on!

Chapter 3

CURSES, SPELLS, AND POTIONS

Q. How does a wizard order dinner?
A. "Expecto pizza!"

Q. How does a wizard find the remote control?
A. "Accio remote!"

•

Q. How does Harry Potter order coffee?
A. "Espresso patronum!"

Q. What spell do wizards use to iron their robes?
A. "Pressed-o!"

•

Q. How does Harry Potter get dressed in the morning?
A. "Expecto pantstronum!"

•

Q. What did the professor who wanted more money say?
A. "Expecto mybonus!"

Q. Did you hear about the wizard who used his wand as a drumstick?

A. He'd shout out, "Expecto drumsolo!"

•

Q. Did you hear about the student who got kicked out of wand-training class?

A. He was expellediaramus!

•

Q. Who are the dimmest wizards?

A. The ones who have been stupefied!

•

Q. Did you hear about the wizard who got turned down for the Yule Ball?

A. He was "rejecto!"

•

Q. How do Hawaiian wizards say hello?

A. "Alohomora!"

•

Q. What do you get when Hermione takes a Charms class?

A. Charmione!

32

Curses, Spells, and Potions

Q. Why did Professor Snape send Harry Potter to the Headmaster's office?

A. Because he was caught cursing in class.

●

Q. How would a Weasley summon one of their brothers?

A. "Abro-cadabro!"

●

Q. Did you hear about the spell Fred used to make George levitate?

A. He used "wingardium levi-bro-sa"!

●

Q. How did Ron gas up the flying car?

A. "Expecto petroleum!"

●

Q. What spell would fight back *Harry Potter* spoilers?

A. "Silencio!"

●

Q. What spell would a wizard need for an anatomy class?

A. "Expecto cadavra!"

Q. What spell does Harry need for bringing firewood to Hagrid's hut?

A. "Accio axe!"

●

Q. What's the swellest potion in Hogwarts?

A. Swelling Solution!

●

Q. Who at Hogwarts has three eyes?

A. Anybody who takes Divination—it's all about the inner eye.

●

Q. What incantation do Hogwarts professors wish was real?

A. "Respecto patronum!"

●

Q. Why did Barty Crouch, Jr. stop drinking Polyjuice Potion?

A. It was making him Moody.

Curses, Spells, and Potions

Q. How would a wizard summon a snake?
A. "Cobra-cadavra!"

•

Q. How does a wizard change winter into spring?
A. "April kedavra!"

•

Q. What's a good spell to use when the WiFi is out?
A. "Connecto patronum!"

•

Q. What do Hogwarts students get when they do bad on tests?
A. Dark marks.

•

Q. Where do wizards go on vacation?
A. Accio-Pulco, in Hexico.

•

Q. Why are essays so hard to write at Hogwarts?
A. Spelling counts!

Q. Did you hear about the Boggart in the charms class?
A. It was Riddikulus!

•

Q. Why was Harry feeling down?
A. He had a bad spell.

•

Q. What looks like Hermione but hates Ron?
A. Draco after he drank some Polyjuice Potion.

•

Q. How do you make Polyjuice?
A. From Polyfruit, of course.

•

Q. Why did Hermione put her wand in a microwave?
A. She wanted to cast a warm spell.

•

Q. What do Death Eaters eat for breakfast?
A. Cruci-os.

Curses, Spells, and Potions

Remember: Wizards who drink Polyjuice Potion are people two.

●

Q. Why did Snape say sad things to his blackberry potion?
A. To make it a blueberry potion.

●

Q. Did you hear that James Potter went to his Yule Ball alone?
A. Yep, he went stag.

●

Q. How did James Potter pick his patronus?
A. With Prongs!

●

Q. Why did the Marauders never forget anything?
A. Because they had a Padfoot to take notes!

37

Q. What's the best way to fight the dark arts?
A. Put up de-fence against the dark arts!

•

Q. What's the difference between Polyjuice and a large body of water?
A. One's a specific potion, and one's the Pacific Ocean.

•

Q. What toy do little wizards play with?
A. Action transfigures.

•

Q. Why didn't the wizard's mobile phone work?
A. Because somebody had cast an "immobulus" spell on it.

•

Q. Why didn't the wizard get invited to the Yule Ball?
A. He never got an incantation.

•

Q. What should you give someone who's been cursed with the Slug-Vomiting Charm?
A. Plenty of extra room.

Q. What kind of drink do magical parrots like?

A. Pollyjuice.

•

Q. "Ascendio" is a spell that starts with A. Can you name one with a Z?

A. The Somnambulist charm makes people fall asleep . . . zzz . . . .

•

Q. Have you ever seen the "Expulso" spell?

A. It's a blast!

Q. Did you hear about the Hogwarts student who got pranked with a skin curse?

A. Now she's an itchy witch!

Q. Would you like to hear an explanation of how the Confundus Charm works?

A. Never mind, it would just get all confusing.

●

Q. Could a wizard do a Feather-Light charm right now if they wanted to?

A. Sure, there's no wait!

Q. Why did Ron get an F on a test?

A. He accidentally cast an "Illegibilus" and the professor couldn't read his handwriting!

•

Q. What does a wizard never forget twice?

A. A Memory Charm.

•

Q. Have you heard about the "Muffiato" spell?

A. You haven't? Everyone's buzzing!

•

Q. Have you heard of the spell that magically blindfolds someone?

A. Probably not, it's fairly "obsuro."

•

Q. How does a wizard light up a dark bathroom?

A. "Loo-mos!"

Chapter 4

Q. What happened when Harry got his first wand?
A. It sparked his interest in wizardry!

•

Q. Did you hear about the first year wizard?
A. He was so new that he thought the Floo Network was on channel 394!

•

Q. How does Harry's owl dress up for Halloween?
A. With a head wig.

•

Q. Where would you find Mr. Scrimgeour, the Minister of Magic?
A. Up on the Rufus!

Q. What's the difference between Dobby and a creepy house in Hogsmeade?

A. One has a reeking sock, and the other is a Shrieking Shack.

●

Q. Did you hear about the magical robot that made jelly beans?

A. Bertie Bot!

●

Q. What flavor of Every Flavor Beans do they not make?

A. Nothing!

●

Q. Did you hear Mr. Ollivander had a daughter?

A. He named her Wanda.

●

Q. How do wizards top a wrapped present?

A. With a Bow-truckle!

43

Q. What holds all of Hermione's books together?
A. Spellbinding.

•

Q. What job would a Marauder be good at?
A. A mischief manager!

•

Q. Where's the best place to sleep in the Forbidden Forest?
A. On a Whomping Pillow.

44

Magical Objects and Enchanted Locations

Q. What's the definition of irritating?

A. Losing your invisibility cloak.

•

Q. Did you hear about the high fees at Gringotts?

A. They're really goblin up the profits!

•

Q. What kind of bread do they serve in the Great Hall?

A. Rowls.

•

Q. Did you hear that Fluffy is really good at making things out of clay?

A. He's a real hairy potter.

•

Q. How would a meeting with a Basilisk go?

A. Fangtastically!

•

Q. What's the worst gift you can give a wizard?

A. A visibility cloak.

Q. What do you get if you freeze wizard money?
A. An ice-sickle.

Q. How do you get into the workout room at Hogwarts?
A. You use the dumbbell door.

•

Q. How much does it cost to ride the Hogwarts Express?
A. Nine and three quarters.

•

Q. Why is the forbidden forest forbidden?
A. Because it's forbidden!

Magical Objects and Enchanted Locations

Two Hungarian Horntails walk into the Hog's Head Inn. The first one says, "Sure is hot in here."
The second one snaps back, "Shut your mouth!"

•

Q. How do you get a mythical creature into your house?
A. Through the Gryffindor.

•

Q. What happened when a witch won the lottery?
A. She went Knuts!

•

Q. What cookies do they serve in the Hogwarts dining hall?
A. Fig Newton Scamanders.

•

Q. Why won't anybody tell you where the Dursleys live?
A. Because it's Privet!

Q. What's the most popular fast food burger chain in the wizarding world?

A. Wandy's.

•

Q. What do the prisoners at Azkaban eat?

A. Lox.

•

Q. What do the Dementors at Azkaban eat?

A. Azkabananas.

•

Q. What do Dementors do on their breaks?

A. Azkabanter.

•

Q. What happened when Harry's godfather broke out of Azkaban?

A. Everything went Black!

•

Q. What's the oldest wand?

A. The Elder Wand.

Q. What magical object would you find at the beach?
A. A portkey.

•

Q. What magical object would you find in a treehouse?
A. A fortkey.

•

Q. What's the difference between Ron's stolen method of flying transportation and Harry's curse?
A. One's a car, and the other's a scar.

Q. How could you describe Harry's life before and after Hogwarts?

A. First he lived under the stairs, and then he had to deal with the stares.

•

Q. What did the angry customer at Zonko's say?

A. "Is this some kind of joke?"

•

Q. What animal feature sounds like a magical school?

A. Frog warts.

•

Q. What's the difference between a flying broom and a magical mode of transportation?

A. One is a Nim-bus, and other is a Knight Bus.

•

Q. What kind of chips do the scientifically-minded Hogwarts students eat?

A. Rufflepuffs.

Q. In what state do Aurors train?
A. Auroregon!

•

Q. How do Death Eaters prepare for a Dementor's Kiss?
A. They pop some De-Mentos.

•

Q. How did the Owl Post director respond when asked for instant delivery?
A. "Owl be right there!"

•

Q. Why did the wizard farmer like raising pigs?
A. For the Hog-warts!

•

Q. How do you relieve being petrified?
A. With a bite of shockolate!

•

Q. Why was Kreacher so critical of his employer?
A. He had low elf-esteem.

Q. What happened when Hedwig lost her voice?

A. She didn't give a hoot!

●

Q. Why did Death Eaters cross the road?

A. The Dark Lord ordered it.

●

Q. What kind of cereal do they serve at Hogwarts?

A. Hufflepuffs.

●

Q. What happened to the sorcerer with an upside-down nose?

A. Every time he sneezed, his hat blew off.

●

Q. Why wouldn't Ron's car move?

A. It got stuck in a quid-ditch.

●

Q. What's on the dessert menu at Hogwarts?

A. Krum cake.

Q. How many Voldemorts does it take to light up a wand?

A. None—he's the *Dark* Lord!

•

Q. Is being a Dementor a fun job?

A. No, it's soul-crushing!

•

Wormtail: Master, can you really rise again?

Voldemort: Certainly, but you may have to give me a hand!

•

Q. What part of a play does Sirius Black hate the most?

A. The curtain call.

•

Q. When is it okay to have a frog in your throat?

A. When it's a chocolate frog!

•

Q. Why was Ron's test sheet blank?

A. He used disappearing ink.

Q. What cereal is popular among young wizards?
A. Trix.

•

Q. What's a dark wizard's favorite candy bar?
A. Bella-Twix.

•

Q. What do Mandrakes drink at the Three Broomsticks?
A. Root beer.

•

Q. What does Harry Potter have with his afternoon tea?
A. The Sorcerer's scone.

•

Q. What do Mandrakes eat?
A. Mandrake's cakes.

•

Q. What line from rap songs do wizards like best?
A. "Throw your wands in the air like you just don't care."

Q. Did you hear about the mailed joke?

A. It was a real Howler!

●

Q. What do you call a cooking pot full of onions?

A. A leeky cauldron.

●

Q. Did you hear about the first year student who turned his best friend into a couch?

A. He couldn't turn him back, but at least he was comfortable.

●

Q. Why is news media such a good profession for Hogwarts graduates?

A. There's a lot of *Prophet*.

●

Q. What happened to the house elf after he was freed?

A. He became very sock-cessful.

Q. What's a good name for a magic owl?
A. Hoodini!

●

Q. What school would magical pets attend?
A. Dogwarts.

●

Q. Into which house would the Sorting Hat place a dog?
A. Grrrr-ruff-indor.

Magical Objects and Enchanted Locations

Q. Why do so many students at Hogwarts get a cold?

A. Because they all have to share a single House Cup!

•

Q. Why do so many ghosts haunt Hogwarts?

A. They like all the big scare-cases.

•

Q. Did you hear about the school for magical ghosts?

A. It's haunted by humans!

•

Q. What kind of flower is good for holding a glass of Butterbeer?

A. Buttercups!

•

Q. What's in the Department of Mysteries?

A. Who knows?

•

Q. What do the internet and Gringotts have in common?

A. Trolls!

Q. How do you avoid tragedy if you're got Salazar Slytherin's old necklace?

A. Locket!

•

Q. Where inside of Hogwarts might you find trees?

A. In the Palmistry class!

•

Q. Why couldn't Dumbledore use his Pensieve?

A. Because he put the memory of where he put his Pensieve in the Pensieve!

•

Q. What did Dumbledore say when the ship from Durmstrang arrived for the Triwizard Tournament?

A. "It's a boat time!"

•

Q. What would have happened had Harry not found the golden egg in time at the Triwizard Tournament?

A. He would have been eggs-terminated!

Q. Where does Dean Thomas keep his wand?

A. In Dean's jeans.

•

Q. How does a wizard find their lost shoes?

A. With a Sneakoscope!

•

Q. What trees grow in Godric's Hollow?

A. Ceme-trees.

•

Q. What's another name for the merchandise at the Weasleys' joke shop?

A. Cheap tricks!

Chapter 5

ALL THINGS QUIDDITCH

Q. How many Quidditch players does it take to light up a wand?

A. Seven. Six to work really hard, and one Seeker to get all the credit.

•

Q. Why did the two Quidditch teams keep on playing after a tie game?

A. They had a score to settle.

•

Q. What do you call two Quidditch players who share a dorm room?

A. Broom-mates.

•

Q. Why did Harry Potter throw up after a Quidditch match?

A. He got broomsick.

Q. Why did all the witches want to date the Quidditch player?

A. Because he was a keeper.

●

Q. Why couldn't the witch travel to the Quidditch World Cup?

A. She *didn't* have the Floo.

●

Q. What's a good name for a great Seeker?

A. Airy Potter.

●

Q. Why can't the Weasley twins be beat?

A. Because in Quidditch, they're the Beaters.

●

Q. Why did the Gryffindor captain recruit so many good Quidditch players?

A. Because Oliver Wood.

Q. What do Quidditch players eat for breakfast?
A. Quaffles.

●

Q. What sound does Harry's Firebolt make?
A. "Broom, broom!"

●

Q. Why was the Quidditch commentator coughing?
A. He was a little Weasley.

Q. Why do Quidditch players use brooms?

A. Because vacuum cleaners would be too bulky.

•

Q. What do you call the most junior level of Quidditch?

A. Kidditch.

Q. What sport do magical sea creatures play?

A. Squidditch.

•

Q. What sport does the Sorting Hat favor?

A. Lidditch.

•

Q. Why did the unauthorized Quidditch game get broken up by the professors?

A. Somebody must have snitched!

•

Q. What happens if you don't properly wash your Quidditch uniform?

A. You'll get a bad Quidd-itch.

•

Q. Did you hear Ron finally got to go see the Chudley Cannons play?

A. He had a blast!

All Things Quidditch

Q. Why did the Quidditch player quit the team?

A. She just thought it was a bunch of jumping through hoops.

●

Q. How does a Quidditch newbie function?

A. By winging it.

●

Q. Are there a lot of strategies for catching the Snitch?

A. Not really—it's a real grab bag.

●

Q. How does Quidditch even work?

A. On a wing and a player.

●

Q. What does flying on a broomstick feel like?

A. It's a magical experience.

●

Q. What song gets Quidditch players pumped up?

A. "I Believe I Can Fly."

Q. Did you hear about the Seeker who tried to cheat with his own fake Snitch?

A. Unfortunately, it just wouldn't fly.

●

Q. What do you call Quidditch played on land?

A. Lacrosse.

●

Q. What would you call an actual game of Quidditch played on land?

A. Complicated!

●

Q. Did you hear Quidditch players can eat their meals in their dorm rooms now?

A. They get broom service!

●

Q. What did Harry use when he lost his broomstick?

A. He used the Broom of Requirement!

All Things Quidditch

Q. What player are Quidditch players most afraid of?
A. The Grim Keeper.

•

Q. What do you get playing Quidditch?
A. Soar.

•

Q. What was Harry when he caught the Snitch?
A. Golden!

Q. What's the object of Quidditch?
A. It's a goal if the ball goes through the hole on the pole.

•

Q. Did you hear about the Quidditch player whose skills weren't what they once were?
A. He was losing his grip.

•

Q. What's another name for Quidditch?
A. A magic show!

•

Q. What's the best and worst thing about Quidditch?
A. The flying . . . and the flies flying in your face.

•

Q. Who are the best Quidditch flyers?
A. The ones who are the most Nimbus.

•

Q. What's one thing you'll notice about Quidditch?
A. Matches really fly by!

All Things Quidditch

Q. Did you hear about the Quidditch game called on account of the weather?

A. It was overcast.

•

Q. Did you hear about the Beater?

A. He threw the game.

•

Q. Why do Snitches like Quidditch?

A. Because they have a ball!

•

Q. What's the most powerful tool in Quidditch?

A. A boomstick!

•

Q. Did you hear about the guy with a raspy voice who tried to play Quidditch?

A. He had a bad pitch.

•

Q. What can ruin a Quidditch game?

A. An awful Quaffle.

Q. Where do bludgers go when they're not being used?
A. With the beaters. They're their bludger lodgers.

•

Q. What's another name for Quidditch players?
A. Flyboys (and girls).

•

Q. On what day are Quidditch games played?
A. Flyday.

•

Q. What do you call a bunch of Quidditch players playing in the sky?
A. A wizard blizzard.

•

Q. What's it called when a bunch of Quidditch players collide and hit the ground?
A. A grounded flight.

Q. What did the wizard say when his broom suddenly stopped?

A. "Those are the brakes!"

●

Quidditch rule of thumb: if you don't have a Brake Charm, you'll probably break an arm.

●

Q. Why did every Quidditch team in the world want Krum?

A. Because he was a proven Viktor!

●

Q. Why did the Quidditch team have to forfeit?

A. Because of an unlawful Quaffle.

●

Q. Did you hear about the injured Quidditch player?

A. She went from catching Snitches to getting stitches!

●

Q. What game trains you for Quidditch?

A. Hide-and-Seeker.

Q. What's a good name for a Quidditch player?
A. Chason.

•

Q. How come both boys and girls can play Quidditch together?
A. Because witches can get snitches.

•

Q. What do Snitches eat for breakfast?
A. Golden Grahams.

•

Q. Did you hear about the Quidditch player who didn't care if he won or lost?
A. For him it was all about the thrill of the chase.

•

Q. What professional basketball team could be a Quidditch team?
A. The Orlando Magic.

All Things Quidditch

Q. What other professional basketball team could be a Quidditch team?

A. The Washington Wizards.

•

Q. What basketball player sounds like he could be a Quidditch player?

A. Magic Johnson.

•

Q. What other basketball player sounds like he'd be a wizard and a Quidditch player?

A. Blake Griffindor.

•

Q. How much does it cost to get into a Quidditch match?

A. A Quid.

•

Q. What did the Pegasus call a bunch of Quidditch players?

A. Amateurs!

Q. What vegetable keeps Quidditch players strong?
A. Quidditch spinach.

•

Q. Did you hear about the tough Quidditch coach?
A. She was very Quid-ical.

•

Q. What did Harry say when he discovered Quidditch?
A. "It's a match!"

•

Q. When do most Quidditch matches take place?
A. In the fall!

•

Q. Where do hurt Quidditch players go?
A. Into Quiddicle care.

•

Q. How do you stop playing Quidditch?
A. You say, "I Quid!"

All Things Quidditch

Quidditch is like baking. You can't do it without Beaters!

•

Q. Did you hear about the shy Quidditch player?
A. She had a fear of public seeking.

•

Q. What is every Quidditch match, regardless of the score?
A. A clean sweep!

•

Q. How do you ask out a Quidditch player?
A. "You're quite the catch!"

•

Q. What's a great piece of advice for Quidditch players?
A. "Seek, and ye shall find!"

•

Q. Did you hear that Quidditch is dumb?
A. Just Quidding!

Chapter 6

FANTASTIC BEASTS (AND JOKES ABOUT THEM)

Q. Who's the coolest magical creature?
A. The Hip-pogriff.

•

Q. Why couldn't the Phoenix go into the restaurant?
A. Because there was no smoking allowed.

•

Q. How did the Phoenix get kicked out of the zoo?
A. He was fired.

•

Q. What's the first thing a Phoenix does in the morning?
A. He rises.

Fantastic Beasts (And Jokes About Them)

Q. What's a male Phoenix's favorite holiday?
A. Guy Fawkes Day!

•

Q. Why are trolls wrinkled?
A. Well, have you ever tried to iron one?

•

Q. What do you call a unicorn's father?
A. Popcorn!

•

Q. Why was the half-man, half-horse so arrogant?
A. Because he thought he was the Centaur of the universe.

•

Q. Did you hear about the Centaur spotting in the Forbidden Forest?
A. Once people found out, it was quite the Firenze.

•

Q. What's a good name for your Phoenix?
A. Ashley

Q. What do you call a Unicorn with no horn?

A. A horse.

Q. What do Unicorns wear?

A. Uni-forms.

Q. What does an Ashwinder do?

A. It winds ash, of course.

Fantastic Beasts (And Jokes About Them)

Q. What did one Basilisk say to the other Basilisk?
A. "Sssssssssss . . . "

•

Q. How do you get a magical creature into your house?
A. Through the Gryffindor!

•

Q. What's the tastiest beast in the world of Harry Potter?
A. Chocolate frogs!

•

Q. What do you get if you cross a "Lumos" spell with a Basilisk?
A. An incredibly long flashlight.

•

Q. What do you get if you cross an Ashwinder with a magic spell?
A. *Abradacobra*!

Q. Did you know that some people have recently spotted a Sphinx?

A. Honestly, no lion!

•

Q. What would you get if you crossed a Yeti with a Basilisk?

A. Frostbite.

•

Q. What does a Centaur put in its coffee?

A. Half and half.

•

Q. What happened when the half-human, half-horse didn't put enough stamps on a mailed letter?

A. It was marked "Return to Centaur."

•

Q. How does a Basilisk show its appreciation?

A. It says "fangs!"

Q. What do you call a group of magical mermaids?
A. Moremaids!

●

Q. Where did the Troll go when it wanted to be a star?
A. Trollywood.

Q. If a group of fish is called a school, what's a group of owls called?

A. Spam from Hogwarts.

●

Q. What city is home to the most magical birds?

A. Phoenix.

●

Q. What do you call a wizard with his hand in a Thestral's mouth?

A. Foolish!

●

Q. Which side of a Niffler has more hair?

A. The outside.

●

Q. Why isn't a Fluffy a good dancer?

A. He has two left feet.

Q. Why was Fluffy so smart?

A. Because three heads are better than one!

●

Q. What did Fluffy say when he sat on sandpaper?

A. "Ruff!"

Q. What type of markets does Fluffy avoid?
A. Flea markets.

•

Q. How does Aragog summon other spiders?
A. He gets on the World Wide Web.

•

Q. What did Aragog do when he bought a car?
A. He took it out for a spin.

•

Q. On what day are you most likely to see Aragog?
A. Websday.

•

Q. What did Dobby do after he was set free?
A. He went and got a job as an Elf on the Shelf.

•

Q. What did Dobby say to get his freedom?
A. "Sock it to me!"

Q. How does Dobby leave a room?

A. He uses the door knobby.

•

Q. What does Aragog do with his free time?

A. He goes fly fishing.

Q. What's a Thestral's favorite day of the week?

A. Flyday.

Q. What do you call an Erumpent in a phone booth?
A. Stuck!

•

Q. What comes after a lightning bird?
A. A Thunderbird!

•

Q. Why are Bowtruckles so loyal?
A. They really stick around!

•

Q. What does a Bowtruckle do when it's tired of you?
A. Leaves!

•

Q. What's the worst part about Swooping Evil?
A. First that they swoop, and also that they're evil.

•

Q. How is a Runespoor like a day of baseball games?
A. It's a triple header!

Fantastic Beasts (And Jokes About Them)

Q. How do you greet a Runespoor?
A. "Hello, hello, hello!"

●

Q. Did you hear about the Runespoor who went to work for the Ministry of Magic?
A. It made a great civil serpent.

●

Q. What do you call someone who can ride a Thestral?
A. An ethestrian!

●

Q. What's a classic good news/bad news situation?
A. Seeing a Thestral. It's good you saw one, but it means something bad has happened to you . . . or is about to.

●

Q. Can many people tame a giant fantastical cat?
A. Many try, but Nundu!

●

Q. What smells worse than a Nundu's breath?
A. Nothing!

Q. What do Biting Fairies breathe?
A. Doxy-gen.

•

Q. How is a bite from a Doxy?
A. Fairy bad!

•

Q. Why did Buckbeak go after Draco Malfoy?
A. Because it was Draco Malfoy!

•

Q. What did the Care of Magical Creatures student say when he found the magical creature amid a bunch of hedgehogs?
A. "Knarl-y!"

•

Q. How is a Knarl like a classroom at Hogwarts?
A. So many quills!

•

Q. Why are Hippogriffs such controversial pets?
A. Because love hurts!

Fantastic Beasts (And Jokes About Them)

Q. What did the Thunderbird say to Newt Scamander?
A. "Can I be Frank with you?"

•

Q. Why didn't the Billywig feel like stinging anybody?
A. It was feeling a bit blue.

•

Q. What do you get when you cross an eagle with a horse?
A. A Hippogriff!

•

Q. What should people call Hagrid?
A. The Hippogriff Whisperer.

•

Q. What animal knows everything about all the other animals?
A. Newt! (Newt Scamander, that is.)

•

Q. What magical creature is the most musical?
A. The Erumpent—it's got its own horn.

Q. What time is it when an Erumpent sits in your chair?
A. Time to get a new chair.

•

Q. Why does Voldemort love Nagini so much?
A. Because she gives him hugs and hisses.

•

Q. Why are Animagi so untrustworthy?
A. They're two-faced.

•

Q. How do you get fur from a Demiguise?
A. With a lot of luck.

•

Q. How do they keep track of the number of Centaurs?
A. With a Cent-sus.

•

Q. Into what Hogwarts house would a Basilisk be sorted?
A. Slitherin'.

Q. What do you get if you cross an Erumpent and an Aragog?

A. I don't think you want to know!

•

Fantastic Beasts from the Hogwarts Zoo

- Harry Otter
- Ron Weasel
- Haremione
- McGonagulls
- Rattle Snapes
- Snaping Turtle
- Professor Squirrel
- Moaning Turtle
- Albus Labrador
- Percy Grizzly
- A Death Eater Anteater
- Rita Mosquiro
- Rowena Ravenclownfish
- Salazar Slotherin
- Helga Hufflepufferfish
- Godric Griffin

Chapter 7

Knock-knock . . .
Who's there?
Harry.
Harry who?
Harry up and let us in! The Dementors are coming!

●

Knock-knock . . .
Who's there?
Sirius.
Sirius who?
Sirius-ly open the door!
Knock-knock . . .

Knock-Knock . . .

Who's there?
Potter.
Potter who?
Potter who saved the wizarding world is who!

•

Knock-knock . . .
Who's there?
Auror who?
Auror you not going to let me in?

Knock-knock . . .
Who's there?
Lumos.
Lumos who?
Lumos be kidding me!

•

Knock-knock . . .
Who's there?
Liberare!
Oh, I see you opened the door yourself!

•

Knock-knock . . .
Who's there?
Neville.
Neville who.
Neville going to give up Harry Potter!

Knock-Knock . . .

Knock-knock . . .
Who's there?
Dolores.
Dolores who?
Dolores Hogwarts ever got was under Professor Umbridge!

●

Knock-knock . . .
Who's there?
Hermione.
Hermione who?
Hermione to remind you that I helped defeat Voldemort?

●

Knock-knock . . .
Who's there?
Hermione.
Hermione who?
Hermione good at these jokes?

Knock-knock . . .
Who's there?
Neville.
Neville who?
Neville you mind. Can I come in?

Knock-knock . . .
Who's there?
Draco.
Draco who?
Draco lot of water. Can I use your bathroom?

Knock-knock . . .
Who's there?
Peeves.
Peeves who?
Peeves me that you won't let me in!

Knock-Knock . . .

Knock-knock . . .
Who's there?
Albus.
Albus who?
Albus look both ways before you cross the street!

●

Knock-knock . . .
Who's there?
Seamus.
Seamus who?
Seamus it ever was!

●

Knock-knock . . .
Who's there?
Remus.
Remus who?
Remus stop meeting like this.

Knock-knock . . .
Who's there?
You know.
You know who?
Yes. AVADA KEDAVRA!

•

Knock-knock . . .
Who's there?
Ron.
Ron who?
Ron for your life! It's You Know Who!

•

Knock-knock . . .
Who's there?
Dumbledore.
Dumbledore who?
Dumb ole door still isn't responding to my charms!

Knock-Knock . . .

Knock-knock . . .
Who's there?
Severus.
Severus who?
Severus waiting out here!

●

Knock-knock . . .
Who's there?
Harry.
Harry who?
Harry up and let me in!

●

Knock-knock . . .
Who's there?
Enid.
Enid who?
If Enid anything, seek out the Room of Requirement!

Knock-knock . . .
Who's there?
Hufflepuff.
Hufflepuff who?
I'll huff. I'll puff. I'll blow this door down!

Knock-Knock . . .

Knock-knock . . .
Who's there?
Dewey.
Dewey who?
Dewey have any Horcruxes in here or not?

●

Knock-knock . . .
Who's there?
Newt.
Newt who?
Newt to this neighborhood, can you show me around?

●

Knock-knock . . .
Who's there?
Tonks.
Tonks who?
Tonks a lot!

Knock-knock . . .
Who's there?
Alohamora.
Alohamora who?
Hey, the door came open!

•

Knock-knock . . .
Who's there?
Hoo.
Hedwig?

•

Knock-knock . . .
Who's there?
He Who Must Not Be Named.
He Who Must Not Be Named who?
I can't say! That's the whole point.

Knock-Knock . . .

Knock-knock . . .
Who's there?
Nox-Nox.
Hey, my wand just went out!

•

Knock-knock . . .
Who's there?
Time-turner.
Time-turner-who? Hello . . . where'd you go?
Knock-knock . . .
Who's there?
Time-turner.

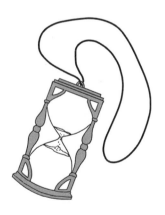

Knock-knock . . .
Who's there?
Guy with a Time-Turner.
Guy with a Time-Turner who?
. . . It broke.

•

Knock-knock . . .
Who's there?
Gryffindor.
Gryffindor who?
Gryffindor is locked, let me in.

•

Knock-knock . . .
Who's there?
Oliver Wood.
Oliver Wood who?
Oliver Wood open the door if he were here!

Knock-Knock . . .

Knock-knock . . .
Who's there?
Nagini.
Nagini who?
Sssssssss . . .

Knock-knock . . .
Who's there?
Severus.
Severus who?
I thought our friendship was so strong that nothing could
    Severus!

Knock-knock . . .
Who's there?
LeStrange.
LeStrange who?
LeStrange you won't let me in!

Knock-knock . . .
Who's there?
Beedle the Bard.
Beedle the Bard who?
Do I have to Beedle the door down?

●

Knock-knock . . .
Who's there?
Fat Lady.
Fat Lady who?
Fat Lady won't let me in!

●

Knock-knock . . .
Who's there?
Accio.
Accio who?
Accio key!

Knock-Knock . . .

Knock-knock . . .
Who's there?
Runes.
Runes who?
You're runes my day keeping me waiting!

•

Knock-knock . . .
Who's there?
Antidote.
Antidote who?
Antidote like it when you blow her up like a balloon!

•

Knock-knock . . .
Who's there?
The boy.
The boy who?
The boy who lived!

Knock-knock . . .
Who's there?
Badger.
Badger who?
What do you mean "Badger who?" You're a Hufflepuff,
aren't you?

•

Knock-knock . . .
Who's there?
Centaur.
Centaur who?
Centaur letters out to all the new Hogwarts students!

•

Knock-knock . . .
Who's there?
Beaters.
Beaters who?
Thunk!

Knock-Knock . . .

Knock-knock . . .
Who's there?
Boggart.
Boggart who?
Boggart *you*!

●

Knock-knock . . .
Who's there?
Buckbeak.
Buckbeak who?
It's me, Buckbeak! Hide me in there, I'm not supposed to be on school grounds!

●

Knock-knock . . .
Who's there?
A magically refilling glass of Butterbeer.
Come on in!

Knock-knock . . .
Who's there?
Rita Skeeter.
Ugh, go away!

•

Knock-knock . . .
Who's there?
Wand wood.
Wand wood who?
Wand wood hope you'd let me in soon!

•

Knock-knock . . .
Who's there?
Confundus.
Confundus who?
Confundus in the Forbidden Forest!

Knock-Knock . . .

Knock-knock . . .
Who's there?
Aragog.
Aragog who?
Aragog to stop wandering into the Forbidden Forest!

•

Knock-knock . . .
Who's there?
Doxy.
Doxy who?
Doxy who fancies a bite!

•

Knock-knock . . .
Who's there?
Crookshanks
Crookshanks who?
Crookshanks you for letting him come in from the cold!

Knock-knock . . .
Who's there?
Crucio.
Well, that's rude!

Knock-knock . . .
Who's there?
Hogsmeade
Hogsmeade who?
Hogsmeade friends too!

Knock-knock . . .
Who's there?
Fawkes.
Fawkes who?
Fawkes who is going to burst into flames at any second!

Knock-Knock . . .

Knock-knock . . .
Who's there?
Floo.
Floo who?
Hey, I wasn't crying!

•

Knock-knock . . .
Who's there?
Keeper of the Keys.
Let yourself in, then!

•

Knock-knock . . .
Who's there?
Howler.
Howler who?
SCREEEEEEEEECH!

Knock-knock . . .
Who's there?
You know.
You know who?
He's dead. You can say his name now.

Chapter 8

Q. What is Lord Voldemort's favorite kind of joke?
A. Riddles!

•

Q. Why doesn't Voldemort have glasses?
A. Nobody nose.

•

Q. Did you hear about the Dementors' kissing booth?
A. There were no survivors.

•

Q. What was Voldemort's least favorite game as a child?
A. "Got Your Nose!"

Q. What do you call an electrocuted Dark Lord?
A. A Volt-demort!

•

Q. How is Voldemort like hand sanitizer?
A. He kills almost everything.

Q. Where do evil wizards work?
A. The Sinistry of Magic.

•

Q. Why did Voldemort collect his Horcruxes?
A. He was getting his life together.

Jokes for Dark Lords

Q. What do you get when you cross the Lord Voldemort with Harry Potter?
A. No more Lord Voldemort.

●

Q. What's evil on the inside and furry on the outside?
A. Lord Voldemort in a bunny costume!

●

Q. Why does Lord Voldemort like hockey?
A. There's always a face-off.

●

Q. How many bananas can Voldemort eat?
A. Avada bananas!

●

Q. What kind of shoes do Death Eaters wear?
A. Horcrocs.

Q. What kind of shoes does Lord Voldemort wear?
A. Tom.

•

Q. What kind of car does the Dark Lord drive?
A. A Vold-vo.

•

Q. Why does Voldemort prefer Twitter to Facebook?
A. Because he wants followers, not friends.

•

Q. Did you hear about the extra-thick pie Lord Voldemort baked?
A. It had seven Horcrusts!

Q. What did Voldemort tell Wormtail when they went bowling?

A. "Kill the spare."

•

Q. How do Death Eaters take notes?

A. With a Dark Marker.

Q. Why wasn't Voldemort at the Yule Ball?

A. He had no body to go with.

•

Q. What kind of books does Voldemort think are funniest?

A. Choke books.

Here's a joke in parseltongue:
Sssss sssss ss ssss ssss?
Sssss sss sss!

•

Q. What do Death Eaters eat for lunch?
A. Death!

•

Q. What happened with *Harry Potter and the Order of the Phoenix?*
A. The books got dead Sirius.

•

Q. What did the woman in love with a Dementor say?
A. "You take my breath away!"

•

Q. What do you call Tom Riddle when he's doing laundry?
A. Lord Foldamort!

Jokes for Dark Lords

Q. What do you call Tom Riddle when he's writing in thick letters?

A. Lord Boldamort!

•

Q. What do you call Tom Riddle when he's on ice?

A. Lord Coldamort!

•

Q. What do you call Tom Riddle when he's been in the fridge too long?

A. Lord Moldamort!

•

Q. What do you call Tom Riddle when he's been canned by a pineapple company??

A. Lord Doledamort!

•

Q. What do you call Tom Riddle when he's been gilded?

A. Lord Goldamort!

Q. What do you call Tom Riddle when he just needs a hug?

A. Lord Holdamort!

•

Q. What do you call Tom Riddle when he's vaulting in the Olympics?

A. Lord Poledamort.

•

Q. Did you hear that Nagini makes really loud sounds when she drinks?

A. She's a real slurpent!

•

You can say a lot of bad things about Lord Voldemort, but one thing he isn't is nosey.

122

Chapter 9

IT'S JUST PLAIN MAGIC!

Wizard TV
The Lone Granger
So You Think You Can Trance
Granger Things
Sirius Black Mirror
Orange is the New Sirius Black
Saved by the Bellatrix
I Dream of Ginny
Draco-La
That's So Ravenclaw
The Dukes of Hagrid
Peeves and Wooster
How I Met Your Malfoy
Mad-Eye Men
Dumbledore the Explorer
Adventure Time-Turner
Breaking Padfoot
Witched at Birth

Witching Nightmares
Fuller House Cup
The Jinx
Perfect LeStrangers
Bewitched

•

Wizard Bands
Phoenix
The Mad-Eyed Moody Blues
Imagine Dragons

It's Just Plain Magic!

Avra Lavigne
The Beedles
Lorde Voldemort
Half-Blood Prince
Tom Petty and the Spellbreakers

●

The Harry Potter Playlist
"Lovegood Yourself"
"Ginny From the Block"
"I Wanna Hold Your Wand"
"Get Leaky"
"Potter in the USA"
"Locked Out of Hogwarts"
"Diadem Young"
"Cauldron Maybe"
"Give Your Hogwarts a Break"
"When I Was Your Mandrake"
"Hufflepuff the Magic Dragon"
"Wild Horcruxes"
"Since U Been McGonagall"
"If You Like It, Then You Should've Put a Spell On It"

"This Goblet's on Fire"

"If I Were a Boy Who Lived"

"Ron the World"

"Da Doo Ron Ron"

"The Sound of Silencio"

"By the Time I Get to Phoenix"

"What Does the Fawkes Say?"

"Love Potion No. 9"

"Row, Row, Rowena Your Boat"

"Can't Be Named"

It's Just Plain Magic!

Q. What's the most powerful candy in the wizarding world?

A. Cornelius Fudge.

•

Q. What movie do wizards watch at Halloween?

A. *Hocus Pocus.*

•

Q. What happened when the wizard was robbed by a non-wizard?

A. He was muggled!

•

Q. What's the difference between a comma and Crookshanks?

A. A comma is a pause at the end of a clause, and Crookshanks has claws at the end of his paws.

•

Q. What's the first thing wizards do in the morning?

A. They wake up!

Q. What did Harry's godfather say when Harry wouldn't stop poking him?

A. "Stop that, Harry. I'm Sirius."

●

Q. How do you get to be an Auror?

A. You have to pass the Auror exam!

●

Q. What's the difference between the keeper of magical beasts and the Boy Who Lived?

A. One's Scamander, and the other's a scar-minder.

Q. What's the problem with Harry Potter jokes?

A. They're riddikulus!

●

Q. What kind of movies do Aurors watch?

A. Auror movies!

●

Q. How does Buckbeak fly?

A. Witherwings!

128

It's Just Plain Magic!

Q. Where did the Harry Potter movie producers find the best actor to star?

A. On a "rad cliff."

•

Q. Who was the most electric performer in the *Harry Potter* movies?

A. Emma Watt-son.

•

Q. What did the actor who played Ron do when he found out he got the part?

A. Rupert Grin!

•

Q. Where is your Hermiones?

A. On your Hermioleg.

•

Q. Did you hear about the death of Harry's godfather?

A. It was Sirius.

Q. How does Sirius take his coffee?

A. Black.

•

Q. Did you hear about Newt Scamander's baking cookbook?

A. It was called *Fantastic Yeasts and Where to Rise Them.*

•

Q. Did you hear about Newt Scamander's album of dance music?

A. It was called *Fantastic Beats and Where to Drop Them.*

•

Q. Did you hear that Professor Umbridge banned *The Tales of Beedle the Bard*?

A. They became *The Tales of Beedle the Barred.*

•

Q. Why did Beedle write all those stories anyway?

A. Because one day he was bard!

It's Just Plain Magic!

Q. Why did James cast a spell to cover his wife in gold?

A. He wanted to gild the Lily.

•

Q. What's Harry's favorite way of moving through the hall of his school?

A. Walking. J.K. . . . Rolling!

•

Q. How did the wizard get to Hogwarts after she missed the Hogwarts Express?

A. She witch-hiked!

Q. Why did Hogwarts have a bunch of surfers try to enroll?

A. They heard it was a boarding school.

•

Q. What's another name for J.K. Rowling?

A. The Merry Plotter.

•

Q. What would you call a mischievous werewolf?

A. A hairy plotter.

•

Q. What do you call a gardener that has a beard?

A. A hairy potter.

•

Q. What would a better name for the last few books in the series be?

A. *Scary Potter!*

•

Q. What would you call having multiple copies of all the books?

A. Very Potter!

It's Just Plain Magic!

Q. What kind of book grows on trees?
A. *Cherry Potter.*

●

Q. What books do cows love to read?
A. *Dairy Potter.*

Q. What books do horses love to read?
A. *Harry Trotter.*

●

Q. What book is best to read on a boat?
A. *Ferry Potter.*

●

Q. What book do wizards read at Christmas?
A. *Merry Potter.*

●

Q. Are reading the Potter books necessary?
A. Harry necessary!

Chapter 10

THE WIZARDING WORDS OF HARRY POTTER

Harry Potter Books From Other Characters' Point of View

- *Vernon Dursley Takes His Creepy Nephew to the Zoo, and He Ruins Everything*
- *Dudley Dursley and His Weird Cousin Who Inflates His Aunt*
- *Severus Snape and the Boy I Don't Like But Have to Save*
- *Albus Dumbledore and the Very Dangerous School*
- *Hermione Granger Saves the Day*
- *Hermione Granger Saves the Day Again*
- *Ron Weasley and the Deadly Game of Chess*
- *My Year in a Turban: The Lord Voldemort Chronicles*
- *Molly Weasley's Guide to Ugly Sweater Construction*
- *Hiding Animals the Rubeus Hagrid Way*
- *Muggles are Neat,* by Arthur Weasley

•

The Wizarding Words of Harry Potter

Wizarding World Anagrams
- "Harry Potter" = "Try, part hero!"
- "Ronald Weasley" = "Yellow and ears"
- "Severus Snape" = "Save pureness" ·
- "Dolores Umbridge" = "Go, Sir Dumbledore!"
- "Draco Malfoy" = "Of a cold army"
- "Peter Pettigrew" = "Tip: Pet we regret"
- "Gilderoy Lockhart" = "The garlicky drool"
- "Arthur Weasley" = "We salute Harry!"
- "Bill Weasley" = "Will ably see"
- "Alastor Moody" = "So moral today"
- "Vernon Dursley" = "Nervously nerd"
- "Lucius Malfoy" = "I, a clumsy foul"
- "Dean Thomas" = "Death moans"

•

Tongue Twisters
- If six slithering snakes slithered up to Slytherin, would sixty slippery slippers stop Slytherin simply slipping?
- Ginny grew up and got rich, and she got rich by catching the Snitch, some say she was the best witch who ever caught the Snitch.
- Filius Flitwick faked out the Fat Friar.

- Ron's wrong, as Granger sensed danger.
- Gilderoy Lockhart locked horns with the horned toad.
- Helga Hufflepuff pedaled past Nearly Headless Nick and almost offed his head off.
- Aurors always ace their oral O.W.L.s
- Peter Pettigrew pickled Potter in Polyjuice Potion.

●

Harry Swifties
- "I'm under the invisibility cloak," Harry whispered, transparently
- "Avada, uh . . . I forgot the rest," Bellatrix said, cursorily.
- "Welcome to the Knight Bus," said Stan, conductively.
- "Meow," said Cruikshanks, categorically.
- "Focus all your attention here," Professor Trelawney intoned hypnotically.
- "Welcome to my stall," said Myrtle, commodiously.
- "The number of students not attending class today really bothers me," said Professor McGonagall absent-mindedly.
- "Looks like my *Lumos* failed," said Ron delightedly.
- "House elves must have done it," Lucius implied.
- "Of course I graduated from Hogwarts," Neville said diplomatically.

136

The Wizarding Words of Harry Potter

- "I was removed from office," Fudge said disappointedly.
- "I teach here," Lupin professed.
- "There goes my turban," said Professor Quirrell off the top of his head.
- "I'll take you to the Yule Ball," Viktor promised.
- "Fluffy bit me," said Hagrid rabidly.
- "The Hogwarts Express is late," Hermione railed.
- "It's the snake, Nagini!" Ron rattled.
- "It's the Mirror of Erised," said Harry reflectively.
- "I'm so full, I could blow up!" said Aunt Marjorie yeastily.
- "Guess where we're sleeping at the Quidditch World Cup?" asked Arthur attentively.
- "The Fat Lady portrait is my favorite," Harry articulated.
- "I wrote *Fantastic Beasts and Where to Find Them,*" said Newt authoritatively.
- "This car can fly!" said Ron automatically.
- "I don't have any hair. It's true," said Lord Voldemort baldly.
- "We need to get Sirius out of Azkaban," said Lupin balefully.
- "I'll get you for this, Potter," said Malfoy begrudgingly.
- "Since we're at the zoo, let's check out the snake exhibit," said Dudley cagily.

- "The Sword of Gryffindor isn't quite sharp," said Neville bluntly.
- "Our prices at the joke shop are very affordable!" said George caustically.
- "Check out these artifacts," said Professor Flitwick charmingly.
- "Hooray for our Quidditch squad!" said Oliver cheerfully.
- "We've taken over the Ministry of Magic," Lord Voldemort cooed.
- "Where's Goyle?" asked Draco crabbedly.
- "I can't wait for school to start again," said Ginny with class.
- "You're going to fail my class," said Professor Snape degradingly.

If you don't get these Harry Potter riddles . . . there must be something Ron with you.

•

Q. When is a dress not a dress?
A. When it's dress robes!

Q. What's the most boring Harry Potter book?
A. *Harry Potter and the Chamber of Commerce.*

Q. What do a Potions pot and Harry's best friend have in common?

A. They're both cauldron.

•

Q. What happened when the wizard was robbed by a No-Maj?

A. He was muggled!

Chapter 11

TOM RIDDLES'S RIDDLES

I wear my hair in a bun
I turn into a cat for fun.
Who am I?
Professor McGonagall

●

My hair is quite red
Don't confuse me with Fred
I got nailed in the ear
But at least I'm still here.
Who am I?
George Weasley

Labeled a criminal,
Into Azkaban I was put
I'm a very good wizard's godfather
But you can call me Padfoot!
Who am I?
Sirius Black

•

I can move you whole, or just one part
Keep your arms tucked in, or you might go to the wrong door
Just a little of me helps you travel more and more.
What am I?
Floo powder

•

I'm really quite small
But I stood up to them all
Until Lestrange's sharp knife
Ended my life.
Who am I?
Dobby

Tom Riddles's Riddles

My studying skills are quite keen
My trips to the library? Routine!
Who am I?
Hermione

●

The Marauders thought I was weak
But then I lived on as a mouse. Squeak!
Who am I?
Peter Pettigrew

●

I t-taught at Hogwarts long ago
Until I d-died one night
When my m-master met his worst foe.
Who am I?
Professor Quirrell

●

I'm a ghost it's true
And I sleep in the loo.
Who am I?
Moaning Myrtle

143

I taught them all Potions
And put plans in motions
All along I was a spy.
Well, who am I?
Professor Snape

•

Not Harry, not Ron
Not Hermione, but me.
I'm the one who delivered
The fatal blow to Nagini.
Who am I?
Neville

•

I irritate newsmakers when I'm out and about
For making up stories and sending them out.
Who am I?
Rita Skeeter

Tom Riddles's Riddles

I'm the oldest in a family of nine
I handle money, but it's not mine
I work in a bank and then joined the Order.
Who am I?
Bill Weasley

●

Do try to befriend us the next time you're in Honeydukes
But please do be careful, we might make you puke!
What are we?
Bertie Bott's Every Flavor Beans

●

I make your teeth shiver
But I'm mostly sweet
Sometimes I have bitter
But you'll probably still eat.
What am I?
Ice-Mice

Saver of lives
Mends bones in a spurt
Hope you don't mind
That it really, *really* hurts.
Who am I?
Madame Pomfrey

•

This place has many rooms
Including the Great Hall
And one time the Weird Sisters
Played our Yule Ball!
What am I?
Hogwarts

•

When playing this game you'd best catch the Snitch
Easier said than done
When you're riding on broomsticks!
What am I?
Quidditch

Tom Riddles's Riddles

I was part of the story from beginning to end
I have many brothers (and one sister)
And I'm the hero's best friend.
Who am I?
Ron Weasley

●

Two hearts longed for me
I hoped for a happy life
It was not meant to be.
Who am I?
Lily Potter

●

I don't have wings
But I can fly.
What am I?
A broomstick

147

I am quite small
And can be rolled into a ball.
What's so important about little old me?
I helped a house elf get set free.
Who am I?
Dobby's sock

Tom Riddles's Riddles

When one arrives at Hogwarts
To this you must submit
I read your thoughts and help decide
Which house will admit.
What am I?
The Sorting Hat

All wizards use this
To cast the spells that they need
A magical tool, indeed!
What am I?
A wand

I'm a terrible place you wouldn't want to come
It's guarded by Dementors
Although Sirius once escaped, somehow.
What am I?
Azkaban

I'm the gruff gamekeeper
And briefly a teacher
I'm part giant and part human
And I sure do love creatures.
Who am I?
Hagrid

●

I am ancient and decisive
And occasionally divisive
Find your name in me
And you'll be competing amongst three.
What am I?
The Goblet of Fire

●

They tried to kill me
And they did with a chop
But my life still goes on
When it should have stopped.
Who am I?
Nearly-Headless Nick

Tom Riddles's Riddles

My normal-seeming outside my purpose conceals
For only to a wizard is my truth revealed.
What am I?
A portkey

●

We're like the Ron and Hermione of Slytherin
We're always with a star Hogwarts student
We're just a lot more sinister.
Who are we?
Crabbe and Goyle

●

You can't hide from me
It would do you no good
For I will always find you
No matter the circumstances.
What am I?
Mad Eye Moody's magical eye

You might find me in your house
But I'm a much more advanced model.
Many may "chase" or "seek" me, but only a few are lucky
enough to employ me.
What am I?
A Firebolt

•

I'm a symbol of loss
And predict a frightening battle to be fought.
What am I?
Harry Potter's scar

•

Seek me out and I shall tell you
What your heart truly seeks.
What am I?
The Mirror of Erised

Tom Riddles's Riddles

I can suit your any want or need
And even hide you
  . . . if *that's* what you require.
What am I?
The Room of Requirement

●

Most people find me a little odd.
It may seem like I've got my head in the clouds
But I'm more tuned in to the life around me
More than anyone.
Who am I?
Luna Lovegood

●

Luna can see us, as well as only a few other unfortunate few.
But don't spook me
Or I'll fly away.
What am I?
A Thestral

I once dated the Boy Who Lived.
Until my pal betrayed Dumbledore's Army, that is.
Big mistake.
Who am I?
Cho Chang

•

Half of me is harmless, and the rest is not
So be careful if you pick me
Or I'll give you an earful.
What am I?
A Mandrake

•

I usually stand still and leave people alone
But don't be so dumb as to challenge me
Or I'll give you a proper thrashing.
What am I?
The Whomping Willow

Tom Riddles's Riddles

We value wit, humor . . . and brains!
Or maybe we're just "for the birds."
Who are we?
Ravenclaw

●

I went to King's Cross when I was briefly dead
I was relieved to be a Gryffindor
There's still a scar on my forehead
Who am I?
Harry Potter

●

Here's a riddle.
Riddle me this?
Riddle me?
I *was* this
And then I transformed.
Who am I?
Tom Riddle

Chapter 12

. . . You looked into the Mirror of Erised, you'd just see a stack of *Harry Potter* books.

●

. . . When your phone says you've got mail, you go outside and look for owls.

●

. . . All you want for your birthday is a broom.

●

. . . Within five minutes of meeting someone, you can determine if they'd be sorted into Gryffindor, Slytherin, Ravenclaw, or Hufflepuff.

You Know You're a Potterhead If . . .

. . . You've taken an online Sorting Hat quiz multiple times and answered the questions differently until it placed you into the house you wanted to be sorted into.

•

. . . You can tell the difference between Fred and George.

•

. . . You knew how to pronounce "Hermione" correctly even before the movies came out.

•

. . . You know that Rowling is pronounced like "rolling," not "row-ling,"

•

. . . You know what the "J.K." in "J.K. Rowling" means.

•

. . . When someone says "J.K.!" you mutter "Rowling" under your breath.

. . . You wonder if an empty hanger is really empty, or if it's just holding an invisibility cloak.

•

. . . You're still waiting for your Hogwarts letter.

•

. . . Chess makes you nervous.

•

. . . You've run into a wall at a train station.

You Know You're a Potterhead If . . .

. . . You like the weird flavors of Every Flavor Beans.

•

. . . You've developed your own recipe for Butterbeer.

•

. . . You've actually played Quidditch (the on-the-ground kind, of course).

•

. . . You routinely use British slang you learned from the *Harry Potter* books and movies.

•

. . . You blame a bad mood on "Dementors nearby."

•

. . . You eat chocolate to make yourself feel better.

•

. . . You talk to the snakes at the zoo.

. . . You've got a magic wand, and you *swear* that it's worked on occasion.

●

. . . You see a traffic cone and think about putting it on your head to see where it would "sort" you.

You Know You're a Potterhead If . . .

. . . You say "Lumos maxima!" before you reach for a light switch.

•

. . . You say "Alohomora" before you turn the knob on a door.

•

. . . You've said "accio!" when your snack is just out of reach.

•

. . . You've referred to school as "Muggle Studies."

•

. . . When you see a portrait, you wait for it to move.

•

. . . You've blamed a poor test grade on a Confundus Charm.

•

. . . You have a pet rat, and you've yelled "Reveal yourself!" at the poor thing.

. . . You can recite Quidditch statistics.

●

. . . Your passwords are all spells.

●

. . . You can dance like a Hippogriff.

●

. . . You call your diary or scrapbook a "Pensieve."

●

. . . You call your diary or scrapbook "The Chamber of Secrets."

●

. . . You call your watch a "Time Turner."

●

. . . You kind of like Ron's sweaters.

●

. . . You've voluntarily lived in a closet under the stairs.

You Know You're a Potterhead If . . .

. . . You call your house "The Burrow."

●

. . . You've taken up reading tea leaves to predict fortunes for you and your friends.

●

. . . You've drawn a lightning bolt scar on your forehead.

●

. . . You've drawn a "Dark Mark" on your hand (just to see what it would be like).

●

. . . Everyday, you've got a different, legitimate need for a Room of Requirement.

●

. . . You poke random bricks with a stick, just to see if it's magically hiding another building.

. . . You prefer a quill and ink to other pens, or typing.

•

. . . You think everything is a portkey.

•

. . . You wish you had a flying car.

You Know You're a Potterhead If . . .

. . . You think Daylight Saving Time is done with a Time Turner.

●

. . . You're a card-carrying member of the Elf Liberation Front.

●

. . . You say "Wingardium Levioso!" when you're on an airplane.

●

. . . You judge everything on a scale from "1" to "9–3/4."

●

. . . You recognize the anniversary of the Battle of Hogwarts as a holiday.

●

. . . You've called someone "Muggle" and meant it as an insult.